The Manse's Voice

To all the
wonderful residents
and staff at
Sandstone Lodge

Kelli Radford

Printed and bound in Canada at McNally Robinson Booksellers.
1120 Grant Avenue, Winnipeg, Manitoba R3M 2A6.

Cover illustration by Agung Trilaksito

Cover and book design by McNally Robinson Booksellers.

www.mcnallyrobinson.com/selfpublishing

First Edition
978-1-77280-132-3

The Manse's Voice

Kelli Radford

Acknowledgments

I would like to offer my sincere gratitude to the Okotoks and District Historical Society, Kathy Coutts, and Marie Wedderburn for helping to make this possible. I would like to extend thanks to Bert and Mary Loree and William Samis for their contributions to this novella. I want to thank my family, friends, co-workers, my awesome Nan, and my wonderful husband who have constantly supported me throughout this entire endeavor.

"I've never dreamed about success. I worked for it." - Estee Lauder

Contents

Foreword

It was June 2016, about a week after my husband and I moved into our new apartment in our new neighborhood in Olde Towne Okotoks that I first came across the most beautiful, fascinating, mysterious house that I have ever seen on 102 McRae St. Upon immediate intrigue and captivation, I instantly wanted to know what stories and tales this house possessed. This rustic structure illustrated a sense of history, memories, and nostalgia that had been waiting for a voice to discover, appreciate, and validate its historical contribution.

It looked olden, yet classic, Victorian; I was instantly attracted to the diamond-shaped square just below the point in the rooftop with four painted upside down hearts whose points linked in the center. It looked as though nobody lived in this house and had not for quite some time. The rocking chair on the front step and the old-fashioned windows elicited in me a sense of childhood nostalgia. The cracked window on the left side of the house and the discoloring of the paint portrayed a sense of abandonment. I wanted to find out who lived there and if nobody did, then I hoped to determine who did in the past.

I asked out loud: "Does anybody even live in this house?" I felt an intense urge to run up the stairs and knock on the front door to see if anybody did live there, but I resisted. As soon as we returned home I searched the address on google. I also searched the Okotoks Archives website and discovered this beautiful house on 102 McRae St. was once a manse for Presbyterian and United Church ministers and their families; it got sold and served as a residential home after 1959. I thought this information would stifle my curiosity; however I continued to feel a compelling desire to learn more.

I wanted the history and stories of the former manse to be told, so that the residents of Okotoks would be able to enjoy and appreciate a written recount of historical information of a property that has stood and functioned as a monument for Presbyterian and United Church ministers for 69 years. The Manse's Voice was created to offer a tribute to the house that had provided a home to many families in Okotoks. If the walls could talk, I am sure they would have a lifetime of anecdotes to tell. I have never been in this house; however, I hope that my illustrations of the outside did justice to the memories and stories of those who once lived inside. The purpose for writing The Manse's Voice was to provide a sense of respect and honor to the former manse and to the people who lived in it who will always be a vital element of the history of Olde Towne Okotoks.

The Search Begins

July 4, 2016

It is my birthday today. I am 41 years young. I went to the Okotoks public library to find information on the former manse. The nice librarian told me about a book written by the Okotoks and District Historical Society. This big book contained a section on the Presbyterian and United Churches; though interesting and helpful I was not sure exactly how I would use this valuable resource that was at my fingertips to interpret the history of the former manse.

At this point, I am not entirely sure what information in particular that I want to show case about this house. Perhaps I could research tales, ghost stories, deaths, murders, births, or stories that would describe what they would say if the walls could speak. I stopped by the Okotoks Archives and Museum next to see if they had any information on the former manse. The young lady at the reception desk gave me the archive's website and said I could find information there. On that website I found a lovely vintage photo of the house, as well as facts that included its construction in 1904 to operate as a Presbyterian manse until it was sold as a private residence since 1959.

July 5, 2016

Today I emailed the Okotoks Archives and Museum to inquire if they had any additional information to offer about the property on 102 McRae St. I hope that somebody could either offer some information or direct me to a source of data retrieval. I am anxious to hear back from someone who has some available information.

July 6, 2016

I received an email from a nice lady at the Okotoks Archives and Museum. She said that they had photos of the former manse and a memoir journal from a lady who once lived there. My husband and I went for a walk this evening; we walked past the former manse and I noticed through the front window that there was an old chair with a crochet blanket on it. It looked like something that my paternal grandmother had in her house when I was a child. I also noticed one window in the second storey of the house was boarded up.

July 7, 2016

I went to the Okotoks Archives and Museum to check out some photos of the former manse as well as the memoir that was written by a lady who once lived there. The Okotoks Archives and Museum had two photos of the former manse. One photo had ladies standing outside in front of it and the other photo showed the former manse when it was once painted red.

The lady who wrote the memoir was Mrs. Elena Young, a Presbyterian minister's wife (Attwood, Young, 1956). Her list of many accomplishments included teacher, mother, and ministry worker. She wrote, about her life from the time she married a Presbyterian minister and relocated from Ontario, Canada to reside in different Canadian provinces including Saskatchewan and Alberta (Attwood, Young, 1956). She described the former manse as a dollhouse and talked about a kitchen fire that took place while she lived there (Attwood, Young, 1956). I took a picture of the page with my cell phone of where she described her time living in the former manse.

Christmas Day was approaching, and there were many homesick young men. Either George or myself (and I hope it was George!) had the bright idea of asking them all to Christmas dinner. The day came, and so did they – ten young bachelors, hungry, and full of good cheer. I have forgotten what we gave them to eat. Possibly George would remember, since no doubt he bore the heat and burden of the day.

I do remember, though, how lovely my table looked, set with my nicest doilies and my good damask cloth, as well as large damask napkins. I believe that we had a very nice dinner, and that everyone had a merry time. Then came the part of the dinner that is graven upon my memory – the washing and ironing of that beautiful linen. Finally it was done, and hung on a line behind the kitchen stove to air, before being put away.

Later in the afternoon, George and I went calling. It was a very cold day, I remember, and dear Simon Peter, with kindly intent, built a huge fire in the kitchen stove while we were away. Alas for my burned table linen! Alas for Simon Peter's good intentions! It was the only time I ever saw Simon Peter abashed, and I thought with sympathy of the peasant woman who once scolded King Alfred so soundly for his carelessness. I have often wondered why history rated her as a shrew.

Although I loved our bachelors, they were no small trial to me, but their hearts were so very right, that I eventually married some of them to my girlfriends in the east, and let them take over my trials. Duck hunting season was one of mingled pleasure and pain. The wild duck and the prairie chicken were abundant and delicious. Roasted together, the result was mouth-watering. A wagon was filled with bachelors and guns, George went as driver at the end of the day, the booty was stacked into our tiny kitchen for the boys to pick and dress. How those feathers flew!

But before they left, the kitchen was spick and span, all the naked little bodies waiting for Mrs. Young to roast next evening for dinner. One night I was too tired to superintend the cleaning up. "Go home," I said, yawning. "I'll do it in the morning." (Elena Attwood Young, 1956, p. 50).

I loved Mrs. Young's vivid description about her time living on 102 McRae St. On this day I also walked past the former manse twice in hopes of finding some construction workers doing repairs on the house who may have some information about the property. And maybe if I turned on some of the old Radford charm that I luckily inherited from two generations, they may let me enter the house to take a few photos.

That same evening, during our walk, my husband and I walked past the manse and saw a cat on the front steps. It came over as if to greet us and followed behind a few steps as we walked away. I stood on a rock outside the fence on the side of the property and saw a door opened ajar at the back of the house. I was, to say the least practically itching to climb over the fence and barge through that door to uncover what hidden treasures and stories this house has to offer.

I went to sleep that night thinking about the former manse and what possible stories it could have to tell. There must be more information or stories recorded somewhere. Of all the Presbyterian and United Church ministers and their families who resided in that house until 1959, somebody somewhere must have a memory or a story to share. I am just yearning to get the stories and tell them, but also to find out why this property is such an uncanny fascination for me.

Retrieved from the Okotoks Archives and Museum, Okotoks, AB

July 8, 2016
Today my husband and I went to the Okotoks Art Gallery, Dit-n-Dat store, and the Bernie Brown gallery looking for books on ghost stories in Okotoks. We were unsuccessful. My husband asked me today if I wanted to go walk past the former manse to get my fix, but I said no not this evening.

July 14, 2016

I have not looked up any information about the former manse lately. I turn my head to the left and catch a glance of the house every morning on my way to work, and turn my head to the right on my way driving home from work in hopes of seeing somebody working outside the house that I could talk to about the property. Two co-workers at the hotel asked me this week if I had obtained any more information about the house, as they have not heard me speak of it in a few days.

I asked my work supervisor today for Saturday, July 30th off, as there is a heritage walk scheduled for that day hosted by the Okotoks Archives and Museum that I really wanted to attend in hopes of uncovering some new information. I showed my boss the picture of the house on my cell phone, and he said he knew of this house as he heard that it was haunted; however, the house he was thinking of was forlorn. In the picture I took on my phone of the house it did not look that way at all. I managed to capture the beauty of this house and interpret my perception of its magnificence.

My husband and I went for a walk today past the house and the cat was on the front porch again. It came over to greet us as usual. Oh how I wish I could just open the gate, walk up to the porch steps, open the front doors, go inside and search for clues to uncover its mysteries and treasures, but the security cameras always manage to stop me. Today I also emailed the local newspaper in Okotoks, the Western Wheel and asked if they had any news articles or photos of the house.

July 15, 2016

It is my beautiful godchild's birthday today. I received an email from the office manager at the Western Wheel saying that they had books and articles that I could browse through if I had any specific dates or events. Though I do not have any particular dates in mind in which to conduct a search, I was happy to get a response. I also walked past the former manse today in hopes that I could meet any construction workers or owners of the house. Unfortunately, I saw neither a construction worker, nor the friendly cat.

After walking past the former manse, I walked over to the Okotoks Archives and Museum and asked the lady at the reception desk about signing up for the heritage walk, but she said just to show up at the meeting place on July 30th. I discovered that they are also hosting a ghost tour in August. I was so excited about this because I figured I could obtain some information about the former manse and I would not have to wait until Halloween to participate in the annual ghost tour. The lady told me to go to the Okotoks Museum and Art Gallery for tickets, so I went there and the lady at the reception desk told me that they were not made up yet, but to come back early next week. On Monday I will go there to purchase the tickets.

After leaving the Okotoks Archives and Museum I went to the House of Proust antique shop in Okotoks. I spoke with this very interesting and classy lady there who said she moved to Okotoks from England about 35 years ago and that her husband is from Saskatchewan. After telling her about the mid-century modern table and chairs that I had my eye on in that store since June, I told her that I was interested in the former Presbyterian and United Church manse on 102 McRae St. She told me that she was familiar with the house, as well as suggested a book that was written by a doctor who once resided in Okotoks called "The Doctor Goes West."

I went home and looked on google and apparently this doctor wrote a couple of books about his time in Okotoks. The book was actually called *A Doctor In The West*, written by Morris Gibson. He wrote another one called *A View of The Mountains*. Unfortunately the computers were down at the public library due to a hail storm, so I could neither obtain a library card nor look up on their computers if they possessed any of those books. What bad luck I had today.

I will return there tomorrow and search for those books written by Morris Gibson to see if there is any information such as dated events or anything that ever happened in the former manse, so that I could check out the archives at the Western Wheel. There are stories and tales of that house that are just bursting to be told, and yours truly is not going to stop until they are uncovered. I feel as though I owe it to the former manse itself, the former residents, the town of Okotoks to uncover their stories and give them a voice. Though luck does not seem to be in my favor at the moment, I will uncover the tales and tell them. A house does not stand for over 100 years without anybody having any stories or memories to be shared; this historical landmark deserves a respect, a voice, an ambassador to recount its anecdotes.

And the Search Continues

July 16, 2016

I went to the Okotoks public library today and checked out three books written by Morris Gibson: *A Doctor In The West, One Man's Medicine,* and *A Doctor's Calling.* This evening I started to read *A Doctor In The West.*

July 17, 2016

I showed two co-workers today the picture of the former manse on my phone and asked if either of them knew anything about it, but they have never even heard of the place. How such a historic landmark could be part of the community for over a hundred years, yet nobody seems to have any interesting information, or even knows it exists is beyond my comprehension. I checked my email after I got home from work today and there was one from the editor of the Western Wheel who did not re-member any recent articles on the manse to his recollection; however he suggested I check out the Okotoks Archives and Museum as well as the Okotoks Museum and Art Gallery. It was nice of him to respond to my email, though I had already checked out both the archives and the museum.

July 18, 2016

Today I got an email from the president of the Okotoks and District Historical Society with a link to the same book that I got from the public library. So far I'm 63 pages in to *A Doctor In The West* and the doctor and his family made it to Okotoks all the way from England in 1955, so hopefully there will be something written about the former manse. In 1955, it was still owned by the Presbyterian and United Churches. Wouldn't it be interesting if Morris Gibson visited that place, the very same one I have been inquiring about since June?

July 19, 2016

I went to the Okotoks Museum and Art Gallery today to purchase tickets for the upcoming ghost tour on August 18 that it is hosting. As I was walking there I glanced at the former manse and noticed in the left window on the second floor of the house that there was a white Victorian looking shirt or dress hanging. I told my husband about it later that evening. We walked past the house to see it up close.

It actually was a white, mannequin body form for displaying clothes. The blinds were closed in the living room and there was a wire-like fence around the side of the house where the basement was being dug out. The cat lazily got up from the porch step to come over and greet us again.

Today I also finished reading *A Doctor In The West*. It was a great book; however, no mention of the former manse was made. Perhaps I will find a story about the former manse in his next book.

July 20, 2016

I started reading *A Doctor's Calling* today also written by Morris Gibson. I hope I can find something about the former manse. Maybe he made a house call there, or somebody who once lived there went to his and his wife's office for medical treatment.

July 21, 2016

My husband and I walked past the former manse this evening on our walk; I took a few pictures of the sunflowers in front of the house. The friendly cat came out to greet us. I looked on the internet after we got home, and I came across a doctor by the name of Grant Hill, who was once a colleague of Dr. Morris Gibson. I might contact him to see if he has any information on the former manse to offer me. Apparently Dr. Grant Hill still resides in Okotoks.

July 22, 2016
I found a phone number for Dr. Grant Hill. My husband thinks I should not bother him by calling. I might write him a letter instead.

July 23, 2016
I finished reading *A Doctor's Calling* today. Although it was a very interesting book and Morris Gibson is a fascinating story teller, there was no mention of the former manse. My next plan of action is to contact Dr. Grant Hill and ask him if maybe he knows anyone who lived in the former manse, or maybe he made house calls there once upon a time.

July 28, 2016
My husband and I went for a walk this evening. We stopped by the house. I took more pictures of the sunflowers. We did not see the friendly cat today. We noticed the white mannequin body form was removed from the second storey window.

July 30, 2016
Today my husband and I participated in a guided heritage walking tour that the Okotoks Archives and Museum was hosting. I previously asked for the day off of work so that I could go on this tour in hopes that the guide would offer some information or stories about people who once resided in the house on 102 McRae St. It turned out that the former manse was not included on this particular tour; however, it is included on another tour given at a later date. Though I enjoyed the tour that we had participated in, as the guide was a wonderful and enthusiastic storyteller, I was hoping to learn some new information about the former manse.

July 31, 2016

Today at work a co-worker of mine asked me about the heritage tour. I told her about how much I enjoyed the tour; however, I did not acquire any new information about the former manse. She said she admired the passion I had for the former manse and my determination to keep digging until I was satisfied enough that I did it justice and to keep her posted on what I uncovered.

August 1, 2016

This morning as I was driving to work I noticed that the white mannequin body form was placed back in the second storey window of the former manse. I was telling more co-workers today about the former manse and one of them suggested the next time I pass by to just knock on the door to see if anybody is there and ask to go inside and look around. I do not have enough nerve to pursue that. So I think I will continue to just walk past it and search for information like I have been doing since early June.

After I got home from work today I emailed contact people for three different seniors assisted living facilities in Okotoks to ask if any residents there would be interested in meeting with me to offer information or personal stories about the history of Olde Towne Okotoks. I offered to volunteer my time visiting the residents on a regular basis in exchange for their time and stories. At this time I am not satisfied with the amount of information that I have discovered. I really want to start uncovering some amazing stories about people who have lived at the former manse, have visited it, died in it or haunted it. What could be more interesting and fascinating than first person, authentic viewpoints in their natural forms?

August 2, 2016

Today I received a response from two of the senior citizens facilities. One contact person said that somebody would get back to me at a later date, and another said she would be out of her office until August 15. That's at least some progress right? This evening while google searching facts about the former manse I came across the name of an Okotoks real estate agent, so I emailed him to inquire if he had any information about the property.

August 3, 2016

Today I got an email from the real estate agent. He said he was sorry but he did not have any information about the former manse. It was worth a try.

August 4, 2016

What is it about this house? I mentioned the former manse today to the hotel owner where I work. I showed her the picture on my phone and she said she is familiar with the former manse's location but she did not know anything about it; however, she did tell me about a website that allows you to conduct title searches on properties for a fee of $10.00.

Today after work I phoned Dr. Grant Hill. I know my husband told me I should not bother the doctor by calling him at home, but I just could not stand it anymore. I really wanted to find some stories about this house. He was very friendly and told me a couple of anecdotes about his time working with Dr. Morris Gibson. I asked Dr. Hill if he could recall any house calls made to the former manse or anybody in particular he knew who lived there, but he could not recall.

This evening my husband and I attended Art on the Lawn at the Okotoks Museum and Art Gallery. We walked past the former manse on our way to the library as I have not walked past it in a few days and had been missing it. How desperately I wanted to knock on the door and ask whoever answers if I could just come in for five minutes to take a look around. The mannequin was up in the window and the sunflowers outside the front gate were tall and bright. I love sunflowers as they remind me of my late stepfather Charlie, god rest his precious soul.

I went to the public library this evening and checked out the book published by the Okotoks Historical Society called *A Century of Memories*. I looked for another book by Morris Gibson *A View of the Mountains*. The Okotoks public library did not have it; however, they ordered it for me. I cannot wait to read it.

August 5, 2016

This evening my husband and I did an online title search on the former manse. We discovered the name of the current owner. He purchased the property in 2007.

August 6, 2016

Today I talked to one of the front desk agents at the hotel where I work about the former manse. She said she used to work at the Okotoks Archives and Museum but she did not have any information about the former manse. I told her how much I loved the house and how drawn I have been to it since I had first discovered it in June. She suggested I contact a tarot reader to find out why.

August 7, 2016

The co-worker, who suggested I get a tarot reading, told me today that she googled the former manse after she got home from work yesterday. She told me to keep her posted on any new information I discover about the property. Another co-worker in the housekeeping department asked me if I found any new discoveries. She also told me to keep her posted. Now everybody at the hotel is curious about this mysterious piece of property.

August 11, 2016

The past couple of days I have been skimming through the *Century of Memories* book that was published by the Okotoks and District Historical Society in 1983. I have read about some families who resided in Okotoks. I will keep skimming until I finish this 650 page book.

On another note, I was talking to this lovely artist at Art on the Lawn this evening. I bought one of her beautiful paintings. She said she has been living in Okotoks for 28 years, so of course I took out my cell phone and showed her a picture of the former manse and asked if she knew of this house. She was familiar with it and like myself, seemed to appreciate its outer beauty. She told me of a name of a gentleman who writes a monthly column in the Western Wheel and told me I should contact him because he may have some information about that property.

So after the event, I went to the Okotoks public library to pick up my copy of Morris Gibson's *A View Of The Mountains*. I emailed the Western Wheel once again after I got home to ask if they could put me in contact with the gentleman who writes the monthly column.

August 15, 2016

Today I received an email from the program manager of one of the retirement living facilities. She asked for my contact information and said she would post it at the facility for the tenants to contact me if they are interested in telling me stories of Olde Towne Okotoks. I was happy to get a response; however, it did not feel promising to me. I think the chances of anyone contacting me are minimal to zero.

August 16, 2016

Tonight I went on the haunted house ghost walk that the Okotoks Archives and Museum was hosting with my husband, my father and my stepmother. It was very entertaining and interesting. Our guide took us to the former manse. There was a light on in one of the rooms upstairs. I was expecting to hear a chilling tale of some sort; however, the guide only told us that this property is believed to be haunted by a spirit in the downstairs bedroom.

There was no information given about the spirit. I did find out the name of the undertaker in Okotoks in the 1930's; his name was John Wilson. That could be some sort of clue couldn't it? I guess I will have to just keep digging for the stories.

August 19, 2016

A co-worker asked me today about the haunted ghost tour. I am now at the crossroads on this search. I have unofficially reached the fork in the road where I must decide either to continue or to stop searching and just let it remain an old manse that is no longer inhabited. I want to keep searching as I feel as though I owe it to the house; however, I am running out of ideas and resources to explore.

This evening after supper I spent some time going through the book *Century of Memories* and discovered that according to the Okotoks and District Historical Society (1983) a Reverend William J. Kidd and his wife lived in the manse when they came to Okotoks from British Columbia so he could serve as a minister to the United Church of Okotoks when the United and the Presbyterian Churches united. As claimed by the Okotoks and District Historical Society (1983) they had four children, Alice, Beulah, Jim, and Billy; Billy was only two weeks old when Mrs. Kidd died in 1924. I wonder, since there were no hospitals in Okotoks during that time, was baby Billy born in that house? Did Mrs. Kidd pass away in the former manse? Could it be her spirit that haunts that place?

Maybe that could be why I feel so drawn to this place. This foundation that is still standing after over 100 years has housed many ministers, their wives and children. This former manse was a revolving door that has seen so many families come and go during the depression years and World War I, and is still standing today.

As I continued reading *A Century of Memories* I discovered that Reverend Kidd's daughter Alice trained as a nurse in the Calgary General Hospital and her son Blair graduated from Dalhousie University (Okotoks and District Historical Society, 1983). Interesting, I trained as a nurse's aide, and I graduated from Dalhousie University. I also discovered that Beulah was a grade two teacher and had a daughter Cathy who taught High School French (Okotoks and District Historical Society, 1983). I was an English Second Language teacher for 6 years and I studied French at Dalhousie University. What interesting coincidences.

Reverend Kidd's son Jim became a district judge in Calgary and had three children; his daughter Margaret lives in Victoria and is married to a Professor of the University of Victoria (Okotoks and District Historical Society, 1983). I used to live in Victoria. Could these coincidences be some clues as to why I feel a need to find the missing pieces of this house's puzzle?

Breaks in the Case

August 23, 2016

Today I emailed, or thought I emailed the present owner of the former manse. There was an email address for a gentleman in Okotoks who has the same name as the present owner of the former manse who is a certification liaison for the board of directors for the international society of arboriculture prairie chapter. I asked if this was the same person who is the owner of a property on 102 McRae St. in Okotoks and if so, would provide me with some information about the house. I hope I emailed the right person.

August 24, 2016

I made photocopies of the pages from the *Century of Memories* book (Okotoks and District Historical Society, 1983). I finished reading Gibson's book *View of The Mountains*. The librarian who was serving me at the counter looked elderly, so I asked her if she was from Okotoks. She said she had lived here for about 26 years so I showed her a picture of the former manse on my phone, but she was not familiar with the place at all. It was worth a try at this point, right?

I composed a letter to the current owner of the former manse today. I asked him if he had any stories or tales that he would like to share with me and I included my email address and cell number. My husband will post the letter for me tomorrow. We walked past the house this evening and the friendly cat walked over to us from the front porch to say hello. After we got home this evening I evaluated the information that I have up to this point.

Thanks to the book *Century of Memories* (1983) the story of the manse began when it was built in 1894 for the ministers who served at St. Luke's Presbyterian Church. As stated by the Okotoks and District Historical Society (1983) Reverend Scott lived there from 1895 to 1899. As claimed by the Okotoks and District Historical Society (1983) Reverend Joseph Ball lived there from 1899-1901. On the authority of the Okotoks and District Historical Society (1983) James Hastie lived there from 1901-1903. As specified by the Okotoks and District Historical Society (1983) Reverend George Young lived there in 1904; his wife provided the journal excerpt about her time living in the former manse.

As per the Okotoks and District Historical Society (1983) Reverend A.M. Rose lived there in 1904. According to the Okotoks and District Historical Society (1983) Reverend M. McArthur lived there in 1905. As claimed by the Okotoks and District Historical Society (1983) Reverend Tate was there from 1905-1907. As stated by the Okotoks and District Historical Society (1983) Reverend J.G. McIvor lived there from 1907-1914. As per the Okotoks and District Historical Society (1983) in 1914 Reverend C.B. Kerr arrived in Okotoks and lived in the manse until 1918.

According to the Okotoks and District Historical Society (1983) in 1917 the Presbyterian Church amalgamated with the United Church. As claimed by the Okotoks and District Historical Society (1983) Reverend William Kidd arrived to Okotoks with his wife Beulah and their three kids as the minister to the United Church of Okotoks. On the authority of the Okotoks and District Historical Society (1983) he lived in the manse from 1917 to 1932. As specified by the Okotoks and District Historical Society (1983) after Reverend Kidd left, Reverend Charles E.A. Pocock arrived with his wife Caroline and daughter Helen lived in the manse until 1939. According to the Okotoks and District Historical Society (1983) in 1939 Reverend J.R. Geeson and his wife Bertha came and lived in the manse until 1942.

Reverend Frank Samis arrived in 1942 from Manitoba with his wife Eunice and lived in the manse until they moved to Medicine Hat with their 2 children William and Lois Jane in 1947 (Okotoks and District and Historical Society, 1983). According to the Okotoks and District Historical Society (1983) Eunice Samis described the former manse like this:

The best feature of the Okotoks manse was that it was heated by gas. One of my first official acts was to turn on the lights of the ornate dining room chandelier. Reaching in to adjust an unlit bulb, I set off a massive display of crackling, flashing fireworks that sent me reeling. The best potential asset of the manse was the large double room, running most of the length of the house, with its central arch. We decided to change this into one spacious, gracious room.

To begin this transformation, I climbed up with my hacksaw and cut down a whole   curtain of Victorian wooden balls and spindles that hung like a harem screen between the two rooms. Later a somewhat startled church board did a thorough job of floor sanding, thereby bringing to view a gleaming new floor of light pine or maple, which well-polished gave us a room where we could live and entertain with grace and dignity. (Okotoks and District Historical Society, 1982, p. 555).

What an interesting illustration of the manse that Eunice described; I could visualize the flickering sparks from the bulb. If I ever did get to see the inside of this property would I see the chandelier or the arch in the large double room that Eunice Samis mentioned? Is that room that the Samis family converted into a spacious room still a one room, or did it later get transformed back into a double room when another family took up occupancy? I wonder what the flooring is now like, or is it carpeted? If I ever stepped inside this house, would I be able to hear the laughter and talking of the people who had dinners, parties, and gatherings that occurred there?

After Reverend Samis left, Reverend J.V. Howey came and lived in the manse until 1953 when he moved to Calgary (Okotoks and District Historical Society, 1983). In 1953 Reverend Bert Loree arrived (Okotoks and District Historical Society, 1983). During the time he resided on 102 McRae St. he married his wife Mary Murphy, a school teacher from Nova Scotia and lived in the manse until 1959 when he left Okotoks to go to

Ormstown, Quebec with his wife and son Robert (Okotoks and District Historical Society, 1983).

Reverend Geeson and his wife Bertha lived at 102 McRae St. from 1939 to 1942; they had three daughters, Eileen, Dorothy, and Gladys (Okotoks and District Historical Society, 1983). I tried to google these three ladies; however, sadly they are all deceased. I googled Reverend Kidd's grandson William Kidd; according to the Okotoks and District Historical Society (1983) he is a lawyer in Ponoka. I figured since he is a lawyer that it would be easier to track down contact information about him.

I found an email address at a firm he works for; so I emailed him to ask if he would be willing to provide me any stories that maybe his father Jimmy would have told him about his time at the former manse. If not, then maybe William Kidd would not mind giving my contact information for his brother Stuart, his sister Margaret, his cousins Blair and Peter MacMillan who would be Alice's sons, his cousins Cathy Rector, Jim Simpson and Tommy Simpson who would be Beulah's children. When Mrs. Kidd died, her youngest child Billy was only two weeks old; he was adopted by her brother Jim Paulin, and his wife (Okotoks and District Historical Society, 1983). According to the Okotoks and District Historical Society (1983) his name was changed to Wm. P. Paulin and he was an executive with General Electric and he was living in Ontario with his wife and three children at the time when *A Century of Memories* was published.

William Kidd would be about 92 if he were still alive today. Maybe his grandson will just think I am a nut case and a complete waste of his time and ignore my email altogether. At this point I am willing to at least try by contacting him.

Possible Dead Ends

August 25, 2016

Today after work I found, or at least I hope I found Ron Hogge's email address, so I emailed him to inquire if he is the son of the late Eileen Hogge. Ron, according to the Okotoks and District Historical Society (1983) was studying architecture at Montana State University. When I googled his name, I came up with a Ron Hogge in Calgary who is an architect. I tried to google Ron's sister's Donna and Lorraine; however I was unsuccessful. There was no mention of Dorothy or Gladys's children.

I tried to find descendants of Rev. Pocock; however, I found the obituary of his son Ralph. According to the Okotoks and District Historical Society (1983) his son Edward is deceased. I googled the name of his daughter Gerry Fisher; however, I did not retrieve any information about her.

I googled Reverend Bert Loree's name and found his brother's obituary. According to this obituary, as of 2009, Bert Loree is still alive and living in London, Ontario. According to a United Church website I stumbled across that is in London, Ontario there was a service in 2014 where they celebrated Reverend Bert Loree's 70 years of ordained ministry.

So I sent an email to that church asking for contact information on Reverend Bert Loree, as I was researching the history of Okotoks, Alberta and I wished to speak with someone who made such a wonderful contribution to the town. There was no information given about his children or grandchildren in *A Century of Memories*. I searched for Reverend Bert Loree and his wife's obituaries and could not find either, so I figured they must still be living.

On google I typed in 'Eunice Samis obituary' and came across her 2008 obituary. I found the name of her son William and his wife Karen Strawn Samis. According to that link, William Samis and his wife are living in Victoria, British Colombia. I found their names on an August 19th, 2012 church bulletin for The Church of St. John the Divine that showed up on the internet whose service included flowers given by William and his wife in memory of the one hundredth anniversary of the late Eunice Samis's birthday.

What amazing things one can find on here. I am so glad I am writing all this down or else I would never be able to remember it all. I also found an email address for the church on this bulletin, so I sent an email to William Samis stating who I was and a detailed note about my project and inquired if he would be interested in sharing any stories about the time he lived in the former manse with his family. I was very busy today.

So as it stands, I am hoping to receive a response from William Kidd, William Samis, Ron Hogge, the United Church in London, Ontario regarding Reverend Bert Loree, and the present owner of the property. I hope that somebody will respond to me.

Finally! A Story!

August 26, 2016

This morning before I left for work I checked my email and low and behold there was one from William (Bill) Samis; it was like Christmas morning to get a response. He told me a few stories from when he lived on 102 McRae St. as a small child. It brought tears to my eyes as I was reading it; finally after over two months of research, I finally got a story about this house. This is what he wrote to me:

I do have a few memories of the McRae Street house. I remember playing on the floor of the living room. It was at the front, in the southwest corner, and I always thought was a sunny room. Later on, Mom commented many times on how cold that manse was in winter. I do not remember that — but she was firmly of the view that the builders had stinted on or entirely omitted the insulation.

I also played on the kitchen floor, which had some kind of linoleum — I was fond of playing with some of Mom's cooking pots, a delightfully noisy game which Dad called "cans and lids" — this was not an activity my parents encouraged, but I managed to fit in the occasional spontaneous session.

Dad had a study on the main floor, and it was always an intriguing place for a little kid. It had a "Winnipeg couch" (a sort of fold-up bed), and a desk which I think was somewhat make-shift. The study was on the east side, with fewer windows than the living room, and was dark and mysterious in a comfortable and friendly way. Dad had lots of books in there, but I was too young to read (particularly theology, psychology, etc.) when we were in Okotoks. However, Dad's desk was full of wonderful things, like pencils and paper clips. Mom discouraged me from going in there, particularly when Dad was working, but he always made me welcome, at least for a few minutes, until Mom came to the rescue, and he usually had something fine to show me.

We often ate in the back yard — summer family meals, and little informal picnics of Mom, my sister and me, feasting on orange slices.

Okotoks was a very peaceful place in the 1940s, but elsewhere the world was at war. There were several military training facilities scattered about southern Alberta, and I frequently saw men in uniform on the street when we went downtown. I also remember some bigger kids doing a marching drill (with wooden guns, I think), on a vacant lot across the street, and I longed to join them — which did not happen. These kids were much bigger than me, and I do not know if they were an organized cadet corps, or just neighbourhood kids marching about. But they carried on for several evenings, and I watched them from an upstairs window in the golden evening light when I was supposed to be in bed.

Also across the street was an old feed store, where the Court House now stands. I think they did a little milling as well. The building was very weathered and ramshackle, but the comings and goings provided entertainment for one who spied through the back fence, or had a better viewpoint from the upstairs window. Most of the feed store customers had trucks, but a there were still a few horse-drawn drays, which I thought very exciting.

We also saw the occasional farmer using horses for farm work, when on car rides in the country — either to Dad's Church responsibilities at Aldersyde, or to visit my grandmother in High River. And in late summer, when we saw a golden field that had been stoked, Mom always pointed it out — as both very picturesque, and as a labour-intensive technique that was fast disappearing in the 1940s.

The Second World War ended the year I turned three. I remember going to see a big parade, which was very jubilant. I am sure I did not understand its full significance at the time, but there were lots of men in uniform. More important, there were lots of big kids (perhaps the same ones who marched under my window) riding bicycles decorated with red, white and blue crepe paper streamers, and more streamers woven between the spokes to make pinwheels — most enviable conveyances, indeed.

My parents took me on lots of adventures around town. Sometimes Dad took me to the newspaper office — usually to deliver a notice about the Church. The editor, who was also the compositor and pressman, was very old and wizened, and had very black fingers. We went to Wentworth's store quite frequently. It was a somewhat old-fashioned general store, with lots of curiosities for a kid to marvel at. One of the women who worked there was always very friendly to me, and gave me little treats when Mom was not watching — I thought this woman was funny looking, and told my Mom, who said it was impolite to say such things about such a nice lady.

The CPR station was across the street from Wentworth's, and in those days regular trains with big steam locomotives were still an important part of Prairie life — and so were their whistles. Dad and I often went over to see the engines, steaming and grunting even when idle, and at least once, an engineer invited me up into his cab to inspect it.

My parents got my sister and me up one night and took us to a front window, upstairs. My sister was still pretty small, a bundle in a blanket. In those days, Okotoks had a whole row of elevators, and one of them was on fire. While it was certainly a spectacular show that is not why we were out of bed. Dad wanted everybody to be ready to go if the fire started to spread and we had to evacuate. Whatever firefighting equipment the town had was no match for a blaze of this size, in the middle of a town of mostly frame houses.

My memories of Okotoks are of a happy childhood. The happiness is genuine and well-remembered — even if my recollection of the details has become somewhat varnished with nostalgia over the decades. – William Samis

Wow! What engaging and epic illustrations of the former manse and of Okotoks during the 1940's. How nice of Mr. Samis to email such wonderful stories. Reading William Samis's email brought tears to my eyes; I finally got the story I have been looking for since June. I could not wait to get to work and tell my co-workers about my email, although they are probably tired of listening to me talk about the former manse at this point.

My entire work place staff probably think I have lost my mind; there were a few times I was starting to think that maybe I had, but the urge to keep searching for someone who knew something about this place was much stronger than worrying about what others thought of it all. I feel as though I owed it to his historical landmark and to those who once lived inside those walls to share their stories. I am the voice of this former manse. If anything is to ever become of this endeavor, I shall title it The Manse's Voice.

I am so glad I listened to my father when he suggested that I try and look up the children who either lived in that house or their parents lived there. If nobody else responds to my emails I will still be satisfied with what I have accomplished for the house, for my own self-fulfillment, and for Olde Towne Okotoks. And I was worried I would never use my research skills that I have acquired while pursuing my Master's degree.

It's Worth A Shot

August 27, 2016

This evening after work I searched online and found a website for a Loree Reunion that took place on July 8, 2011 in Burlington, Ontario. I found an email address for Robert Loree. According to Okotoks and District Historical Society (1983), Robert Loree was Reverend Bert Loree's first child and he was born in Okotoks while he and his wife Mary were living at the manse. I emailed Robert and asked if he had any memories of living on 102 McRae St. that he would like to share with me that I would love to hear them. I hope I hear from either him or his father.

To get more interesting stories from the actual person who had the experience, there is nothing more fascinating. Authenticity is golden.

This evening I emailed William Samis to thank him for sharing his stories with me. I forwarded a recent picture of the former manse and I sent him the link for *Century of Memories* and told him what pages that the picture of him with his mom as a little boy and the picture of his sister as a little girl with their dad are on. How would I ever have done all of this without the internet?

August 29, 2016

Today I received an email from the certified arborist. He told me he was sorry that he was not the current owner of the former manse. He said that people often confuse him with the former manse owner as they both have the same name.

September 1, 2016

This evening my husband and I went for a walk. We passed by the former manse, as I was hoping to see the cat again. We did not see the friendly cat; however, we saw another cat napping on the fence. Why do cats like to hang around outside this property?

September 2, 2016

Today I wrote a letter to the present owner's residential address. I am worried that he would not receive the letter that I had addressed to the former manse. Perhaps he rarely checks that mail box. I am sort of at a standstill now. I am waiting for responses from people.

Have I found all that I am supposed to know about the house? Is that all there is? Where do I go from here? Have a paid sufficient tribute to this house?

The Phone Interview

September 7, 2016

I am so excited! I just got an email from the church administrator regarding Reverend Loree. She told me that the Loree's did not have an email address but gave me their phone number and said that Mary would be happy to talk to me. This is so exciting. I wonder when should I call and what questions should I ask her?

September 9, 2016

I thought of a few questions to ask Mrs. Loree when I call.

1) What year did you arrive in Okotoks? When did you first meet your husband?

2) Could you provide a picture of what Okotoks was like when you first arrived?

3) What was your first impression of the manse on 102 McRae St.?

4) Do you have any good stories about the former manse?

5) Do you have any memories about Okotoks that stand out?

September 11, 2016

Today after work I called Mrs. Loree. She answered the phone and we talked for about an hour and a half. It turned out that Dr. Morris Gibson delivered her first born child Robert in the High River hospital and she attended a big party the town held for him at Sheep River when he first arrived in Okotoks. She did not have a lot of stories about living in the former manse, except for she taught at a school across the street from it. She said it had no basement and they used space heaters to keep warm.

Her daughter lives in Calgary and is a singer and songwriter who wrote the song 'Insensitive' for Canadian singer Jann Arden. She said that the next time she and Mr. Loree visit Alberta that she would contact me so we could meet. That would be interesting and such an honor to meet with two people who were such important pillars in the community of Okotoks.

Though she could not recall any memories of the manse that stood out in her mind as Mr. Samis did, it was interesting and appreciative just the same to gain her perspective of Okotoks when she first arrived here in 1955 for a teaching position. She ended up meeting her future husband and having three children. She said she did not want to leave Okotoks; however Reverend Loree's work brought them to Quebec. It turned out I did not need to feel nervous talking to her or use my scripted questions. She totally ran the show; I was truly grateful for her time and input.

She asked me if I was doing similar research of my family history. I told her no, but this endeavor of researching 102 McRae St. was certainly inspiring me to consider that in the future. She sounded so vibrant, energetic and spry. Mary Loree asked me if my interest in the former manse was perhaps due to the possibility that I lived in a house that looked similar to it. I replied that I did not recall living in anything similar to the former manse.

It was fascinating to hear about when she first arrived here and she kept referring to Elizabeth Street as Main Street, and how there were no paved roads when she arrived to Okotoks. She described it as a 'cow town.' I really enjoyed hearing about her friends she met here such as Myna Noble who she visited at rainbow ranch.

According to Mary Loree, she first arrived in Okotoks in 1955 to work as a teacher. Her roster of students included Cowboy Bill Flett whom she taught fifth grade. He became a successful professional hockey player whose career involved playing in the National Hockey League for the Los Angeles Kings, the Philadelphia Flyers, the Toronto Maple Leafs, and the Edmonton Oilers.

One year while she was living in the manse, the storekeeper, who owned a grocery store across the street from the manse, gave her and Mr. Loree a turkey; they did not know what to do with it, so they took it to the store and the storekeepers took off the feathers for them and prepared it to be cooked.

I never thought I would ever have a conversation where someone would tell me about living in a town in the past, and that I would recount to that individual about present life in that town. It felt so surreal. What an amazing experience!

I also got an email today from Darell Loree. He did not exactly state how he is related to the family; however, he got my contact information from Bob Loree, who turned out not to be Bert and Mary's son. Perhaps I emailed a relative of the Loree family instead of their son.

Where To Go From Here

September 19, 2016

Last night I had a dream that the owner of the house emailed me and said that after he finished renovating the house that he would let me go inside and take a look. I hope that dream becomes a reality. I emailed Darell Loree back today to thank him for responding to my email.

March 13, 2017

Wow, has it really been that long since I last wrote about my beloved former manse? Apparently yes. After I spoke with the lovely Mrs. Loree, I felt as though my research I conducted had run its course. I have often thought about the former manse these past six months, though I have not walked past it lately due to the cold winter weather.

I did not have any plans on which direction I should go in terms of the former manse. I did not have any interest for some reason to try to locate the names of anyone who lived there after 1959. Instead I decided to explore exactly why I am so interested in this property.

I recalled last fall when I spoke with Mrs. Loree that she asked if maybe I felt connected to the former manse because I lived in a house similar to it. I did not think that was accurate at the time. I just dismissed that notion.

For the last six months I have been racking my brain, trying to link the former manse to somewhere I had lived in my past. I thought about every house, apartment and basement suite I have ever lived in from my earliest memories until the present. None of them have the slightest resemblance to the former manse.

I called my Nan today and asked her about the very first house I lived in when I was a baby. I was surprised when she confirmed that I lived in a house that had two storeys. My uncle owned a convenience store in the lower level and my mom and dad lived in the apartment upstairs of this two storey house. I lived in that house from the time my mom took me home from the hospital in 1975 until we moved to a duplex. The duplex is the first place that I remember living in.

My Nan said that the house is now used as an office building and the upstairs is an apartment rental unit on 57 St. Clare Ave. in Stephenville, Newfoundland. The picture I found on google of the house on 57 St. Clare Ave. has a slight resemblance to the former manse on 102 McRae St. My husband said he remembered it was once a dark red color. What a coincidence, just like the former manse was once a deep red color.

I told my Nan that I was hoping to find out my connection to this house. I also told her that I hoped to publish what I found so that one day when my beautiful and mysterious manse is no longer standing, the inhabitants of Okotoks and those who move here after them will know what once stood proud and tall on McRae St. for so many years. I refuse to let it go down as just some old house that nobody had lived in for years. I also promised my Nan the very first paperback copy of my publication of The Manse's Voice to be mailed to her. I hope I am not promising something to Nan that I will never ever be able to deliver.

April 9, 2017

Last evening I was at my dad's house for his birthday. I was telling him and his lovely wife about the resemblance between the house on 102 McRae St. and the one that I lived in when I was a baby on 57 St. Clare Avenue. I showed them a picture of both houses and they agreed with me that they have a slight resemblance to each other.

April 12, 2017

I was finally inside my favorite house! Well, sort of. Last night I had a dream that I finally got an invitation to go inside the former manse and look around. It was magical!

I felt the presence of ghosts. I remember seeing a door slowly open as if the wind was blowing, and it made a loud, creepy creaking noise. The only thing was there were no open windows in the room that I was in.

There were two storeys in the house, hard wood floors, high ceilings, big spiraling stair cases and an attic. There were a lot of bathrooms in that house. I had a dream that I was working as a cleaning lady. There were a lot of bedrooms in that house as well and an attic. I wanted to go up the ladder and see what was in the attic, but I had to work and clean all the bathrooms and bedrooms.

When I was finished, my actual work supervisor was in my dream and he sent me back to clean this one bathroom in the down stairs area with a bedroom off to the side of it, because he said it was not clean enough. When he showed me the areas that were not properly cleaned, I realized that they were not cleaned at all because I had no idea that bathroom existed, as the door to it was slightly hidden in the wall. Then a couple of girls from work started helping me clean it. After that I do not remember the rest of the dream. Maybe my alarm clock woke me up, or maybe I started to dream about something else. I really do hope that my dream is not the only way I am ever going to see the inside of that house.

April 22, 2017

My husband and I walked past the former manse today. It appears that they are putting new windows in the back of the house. I was happy to see that, as it is a good sign that they are still fixing it up. Maybe the owner is fixing it up to sell and he will have an open house one day and I can finally go inside to have a look.

Summary

April 24, 2017

After about ten months of research that involved showing a picture of the former manse to every new person I met, participating in walking tours, reading books, offering to volunteer at seniors citizen's facilities, as well as writing letters, emailing, and calling people whom I have never met, I have struggled to write a conclusion on the positive outcome of this journey. I strongly feel as though I have successfully uncovered the mystery as to why I have become so emotionally attached and invested in uncovering stories of the families who have once resided there, as well as discovered that I once lived in a house that looked somewhat similar that which I hold no memories. The manse on 102 McRae St. was a home for many Presbyterian and United Church ministers and their families. The former manse is a part of Olde Towne Okotoks and will remain so for many more years to come.

The house on 102 McRae St. in Okotoks, Alberta possesses a lifetime of stories; for 69 years this former manse has welcomed and provided a home for new comers to Okotoks to serve as Presbyterian and United Church ministers. Inside its walls are centuries of stories that include love found for Reverend Bert Loree. It is where Reverend Kidd grieved the loss of his wife; his children suffered the loss of their mother. The former manse is where newborns Robert Loree and Lois Jane Samis first lived upon entrance into this world. It was a transient structure that became a home for ministers and their families during transition from their previous domain to the next chapter of their lives until 1959.

It holds the story of William Samis eating a picnic of orange slices in the backyard with his mother Eunice and his sister Lois Jane. It contains the story of Mr. and Mrs. Young hosting dinner parties to a guest list which included eligible bachelors eating wild duck and roasted chicken using her damask napkins. It includes the story of Kelli Radford, who walked past the former manse in early June 2016 and felt an instant sense of affection and determination to unravel the stories from inside its walls.

I hope that many readers will enjoy a publication of stories of the former manse told by some of the families who once lived there. I also wish that my story of how I unveiled the tales of the manse will be amusing and entertaining. By virtue of perseverance, determination, passion, and a strong desire to discover the stories and narrate them, it is through their interpretations that I provided the manse with a voice.

Sources

Okotoks and District, (1983). *A Century of Memories*, Okotoks, AB: Okotoks and District Historical Society.

Young, Elena, Attwood. (1956). *I Remember*, Self-published.

Gibson, Morris. (1983). *A Doctor in the West*, Don Mills, Ontario: Collins Publishers.

Gibson, Morris, (1983). *A View of the Mountains*, Toronto, Ontario: Collins Publishers.

Gibson, Morris, (1984). *One Man's Medicine*, Toronto, Ontario: Collins Publishers.

Gibson, Morris. (1986). *A Doctor's Calling*, Vancouver, BC: Douglas & McIntyre Ltd.